Mystery of the Missing Luck

Jacqueline Pearce

ILLUSTRATIONS BY

Leanne Franson

ORCA BOOK PUBLISHERS

In memory of my two grandmothers. —*J.P.*

Library and Archives Canada Cataloguing in Publication

Pearce, Jacqueline, 1962-
Mystery of the missing luck / Jacqueline
Pearce ; illustrated by Leanne Franson.
(Orca echoes)

Issued also in electronic format.
ISBN 978-1-55469-396-2

I. Franson, Leanne II. Title. III. Series: Orca echoes
PS8581.E26M98 2011   JC813'.6   C2010-907914-0

First published in the United States, 2011
Library of Congress Control Number: 2010941920

Summary: When Maneki Neko, a Japanese lucky cat statue, goes missing from her
grandmother's bakery, Sara resolves to track it down and help restore the bakery's good fortune.

Orca Book Publishers gratefully acknowledges the support for its publishing programs
provided by the following agencies: the Government of Canada through the Canada Book Fund
and the Canada Council for the Arts, and the Province of British Columbia
through the BC Arts Council and the Book Publishing Tax Credit.

MIX
Paper from
responsible sources
FSC™ C011825
www.fsc.org

*Orca Book Publishers is dedicated to preserving the environment and has printed this book
on paper certified by the Forest Stewardship Council.*®

Typesetting by Jasmine Devonshire
Cover artwork and interior illustrations by Leanne Franson
Author photo by Danielle Naherniak

ORCA BOOK PUBLISHERS
PO BOX 5626, STN. B
VICTORIA, BC CANADA
V8R 6S4

ORCA BOOK PUBLISHERS
PO BOX 468
CUSTER, WA USA
98240-0468

www.orcabook.com
Printed and bound in Canada.

14 13 12 11 • 4 3 2 1

CHAPTER ONE
Missing

Every day after school Sara walked to her grandmother's bakery. Her long black ponytail swung as she skipped down the last block. At the bakery, she always paused to look through the window at Maneki Neko, the lucky cat statue. The statue sat in the window display beside a basket of round golden buns. *Come inside*, the cat's raised paw beckoned.

Each time Sara stepped through the door, she gave the lucky cat a secret wave. The smell of freshly baked buns always made her mouth water. Her favorite was a soft, sweet *an-pan* filled with fudgy red-bean paste.

Today, however, something was different. The round golden buns were in their basket as usual, but there was no Maneki Neko.

Sara pushed open the bakery door. "Where is Maneki Neko?" she asked Obaachan. Obaachan was Sara's Japanese grandmother. She stood behind a long counter with a glass front. More buns and pastries were lined up behind the glass.

Usually Obaachan smiled broadly when Sara arrived. But this afternoon her round face was long and sad. "Gone," she said. "Maneki Neko is gone."

"What do you mean?" Sara asked. How could the lucky cat statue be gone? It had come all the way from Japan with her grandmother years ago.

"When I opened the bakery this morning, Maneki Neko wasn't there," Obaachan said, waving her hands in dismay.

"Did someone steal him?" Sara asked.

Obaachan frowned. "I don't think so," she said. "Why would anyone take an old cat statue?"

"Is Maneki Neko valuable?" Sara asked.

"Only to our family," said Obaachan. "It used to bring the bakery good luck. But not so much anymore."

Sara knew the bakery was no longer doing well, but she did not think it was Maneki Neko's fault.

"Did you move him?" Sara asked. She scanned the room, hoping to see Maneki Neko's pointed ears peeking out from behind a row of buns.

"No, I don't think so," Obaachan said.

Sara sighed. Obaachan had been forgetful lately. She patted her grandmother's hand and smiled. "Don't worry," she said. "We'll find him."

CHAPTER TWO
The Search

The bell above the bakery door jangled. An old woman with curly gray hair entered. She had been a regular customer for years.

"Good afternoon," Obaachan said.

"I see you have your granddaughter helping today," the woman said. She gave Sara a friendly nod.

Sara said hello to the woman. She liked Obaachan's regular customers. There just were not enough of them. The bakery needed new customers too. Sara was sure if more people knew how good Obaachan's buns were, the bakery would be busy all day long. But Sara couldn't think about the bakery now. She had to find Maneki Neko.

Sara pictured the statue. The black paint had worn off where people had rubbed his head and body for good luck. Brown clay showed through the worn patches. *Maneki* meant *beckoning*, and *neko* meant *cat* in Japanese. Sara knew there were lots of beckoning cat statues in Japan. But her grandmother's Maneki Neko felt special. His raised paw always seemed to call especially to her. She looked at the empty spot in the bakery window. Where could Maneki Neko be?

Sara crouched down and looked under the display counter. There was nothing there—not even any dust. Obaachan swept the bakery every night. She must have done a very good job the night before.

Sara searched around the cash register. She looked on the shelf where Obaachan kept stacks of paper bags and cardboard that folded into boxes. There was no sign of the lucky cat.

"Can you hand me one of those boxes, please?" Obaachan asked her.

Sara lifted a piece of cardboard off the shelf. She folded it into a box before passing it to her grandmother. Using a little square of paper to pick up each bun, Obaachan carefully placed the customer's order into the box. Then she closed the top and tied a red string around it.

Once the woman had left the store, Sara excused herself. She went into the kitchen behind the bakery. She searched the tall ovens where Obaachan baked the buns early each morning. She checked the cooling racks and the washing-up area. She looked on top of the little table where Obaachan drank her morning tea. She climbed the narrow stairway to the second floor and searched the small apartment where Obaachan lived above the bakery.

There was no sign of the lucky cat anywhere.

Sara plodded back down the stairs. Where could Maneki Neko be?

"No luck?" Obaachan asked when Sara came back into the bakery.

Sara shook her head. She glanced around. No new customers had come in since the old woman had left. Sara's eyes went to the place where Maneki Neko usually sat. There was no lucky cat to beckon customers inside.

"The cat will turn up," Obaachan said. "You'll see." She smiled at Sara. It was not her big round-cheeked smile, but it made Sara feel a bit better.

Obaachan held out a plate with a round golden an-pan on it. Sara's mouth began to water.

CHAPTER THREE
Night Visitor

Sara stayed with Obaachan that night to keep her grandmother company. She loved the little apartment above the bakery. It was always warm and cozy and smelled of freshly baked buns.

Tonight Sara lay in the spare bed, staring up at the dark ceiling. She missed Maneki Neko, and even more, she missed Obaachan's round-cheeked smile. Sara knew it wasn't only the missing statue that was upsetting her grandmother. Obaachan was concerned about the bakery. If it continued to lose money, she would have to shut it down. Sara thought if she could find Maneki Neko, everything would be all right.

Sara had been asleep for a while when something woke her. Her heart pounded. Had she heard a bump downstairs? Maybe someone *had* stolen the lucky cat, and now the thief was back. She held her breath and listened. But all she could hear was Obaachan's soft snoring coming from the next room. Sara tried to fall back asleep but couldn't. She climbed out of bed and tiptoed across the floor to the window. The window looked out over a small backyard. Sara pulled aside the curtain and pressed her face close to the glass. Was someone out there?

At first she could see nothing but darkness and shadows and the dark shape of a cherry tree. Then a small movement caught her eye. A shadow poured away from the tree. But it was not a shadow. It was a cat.

The cat padded lightly into the middle of the yard and sat in a puddle of moonlight. Paying no attention to Sara, it licked one paw and began to wash itself. There was something both familiar and mysterious about the cat. Its lifted paw reminded

Sara of her grandmother's statue, but this was no statue. Sara guessed it must be someone's pet.

Sara stared sleepily out the window. Her nose clunked against the glass. The cat stopped cleaning itself and looked up. The cat's eyes met Sara's. Sara noticed the cat was not completely black after all. It had patches of brown on its head and sides. Sara wished she could get a closer look, but the cat turned and was gone.

CHAPTER FOUR
Jake

The next morning Maneki Neko had still not turned up, and Obaachan seemed troubled. Sara wished there was something she could do to help the bakery.

At school Sara sat at her desk in her grade-two classroom, staring out the window. She opened her lunch without looking at it.

"What's that?" asked Jake. He sat in the desk beside Sara. Up close, she could see the brown freckles sprinkled across his nose. He had already started eating his lunch. There was a dab of yellow mustard on his chin.

Sara looked at the plastic container on her desk. In it was a long bun with holes cut into the top to reveal the filling inside.

"It's a peekaboo bun," Sara told Jake. It was one of the buns Sara had helped her grandmother name. "It has ham, cheese and egg inside."

"Cool," Jake said, peering closer. "It looks like it has windows."

Sara grinned. That's what she had thought too.

"My grandma made it," she said. "Do you want a piece?"

She tore off one end of the bun and passed it to Jake.

"Thanks," he said, taking a bite. "This is good!"

"Yeah," Sara agreed. Everything Obaachan made was good. It would be awful if the bakery had to close.

"You should come visit my grandma's bakery sometime," she said to Jake.

Jake's mouth was full, and he mumbled something that sounded like "Okay." Sara wasn't sure.

But it didn't matter. Even if one new person came to the bakery, it wouldn't be enough.

After school Sara walked slowly back to the bakery. For the first time, she wasn't looking forward to arriving at Obaachan's. She didn't want to see the empty spot where Maneki Neko used to sit.

"Hey, wait for me!" a voice called from behind her.

She turned to see Jake hurrying to catch up.

"Are you going to your grandma's bakery?" he asked. "Can I come?"

Sara laughed. Jake was always hungry.

CHAPTER FIVE
Japanese Buns

As they approached the bakery, Sara's heart beat faster.

"Is this it?" Jake asked when they stopped.

Sara didn't hear him. She stared at the bakery window, holding her breath. Was the lucky cat there?

Sara's shoulders dropped and her breath whooshed out like a deflating balloon. Maneki Neko's spot was still empty.

"What's wrong?" Jake asked.

Sara told him about the missing statue.

"Maybe it will turn up," Jake said.

Sara pushed open the door, and Obaachan looked up from behind the counter.

"This is my friend Jake from school," Sara told her grandmother.

Obaachan's cheeks broadened into a welcoming smile. Sara was glad Jake had come.

"I saved you some an-pan," Obaachan said. "Something told me to save two. Now I know why." She turned and disappeared through the curtained door at the back of the bakery.

Jake peered hungrily at the rows of Japanese buns and pastries.

"What's that?" he asked, pointing at a round puffy pastry with something thick and green oozing out.

"A green-tea cream puff," Sara said.

Jake wrinkled his nose, and Sara laughed.

"It's good," she said. "Really."

Jake looked up from the display case and glanced around the room.

"Is your grandma the only one who works here?" he asked.

"Yeah," Sara said.

"Does she go into the back often?"

Sara shrugged. "I don't think so."

"It would be pretty easy for someone to come in and steal something if she wasn't here," Jake said.

Sara narrowed her eyes. "You think that's what happened to the lucky cat?" she asked.

"Maybe," he said. "Or someone left the door open, and it walked out on its own."

"Very funny." Sara glared at him.

Obaachan returned, carrying a black tray with a teapot, cups and two round buns on plates.

"Are those hamburgers?" Jake asked.

"No." Sara laughed. "They're an-pan." She explained about the sweet bean-paste filling.

Jake thanked Obaachan and picked up one of the buns. He eyed it doubtfully.

20

"*Pan*. Is that like the French word for bread?" Jake asked.

"It sounds like it," Sara said. "But the Japanese *pan* comes from a Portuguese word, I think." She looked at Obaachan.

"Yes," her grandmother said. "Bread was brought to Japan by Europeans, but Japanese bakers make it a bit differently."

Jake took a small bite of his an-pan.

"It's good," he said with some surprise. He took a bigger bite.

When Sara finished her an-pan, she was full. When Jake finished his, his eyes went right back to the display case.

"Would you like to try something else?" Obaachan asked Jake.

Sara wished Obaachan had made her special animal-shaped buns. Jake would like those, for sure. But now that business was slow, Obaachan didn't make as many things as she used to.

"What about a chocolate one?" Jake asked. He pointed to a row of buns that were overflowing with chocolate cream.

CHAPTER SIX
Missing Luck

After they finished their snack, Sara took Jake to the kitchen. She showed him the tall baking ovens and cooling racks. Then they climbed the stairs to the apartment above the bakery.

"Do you want to play a board game?" Sara asked Jake.

"Okay," Jake said. "But something that doesn't take as long as Monopoly."

They played checkers for a while, then switched to Yahtzee. Jake complained that adding the numbers was too much like schoolwork, until he started winning.

"You seem to have all the luck today," Sara told Jake. She wondered if all her luck had disappeared with Maneki Neko.

When it was time for Jake to go, Obaachan was closing the bakery. She gave him a big bag full of leftover buns and pastries to take home.

"They won't sell now," Obaachan said.

"Not many customers today?" Sara asked quietly.

Obaachan shook her head, and Sara wished she hadn't asked. Jake's visit seemed to have cheered her grandmother up. But Sara guessed Obaachan was thinking of the lost luck again.

After they locked up the bakery, Sara and Obaachan climbed the stairs to the apartment. As they neared the top, Obaachan took hold of Sara's arm.

"Are you okay, Obaachan?" Sara asked, looking at her grandmother with concern.

"Don't worry, Sara-chan," Obaachan said, patting Sara's hand. "I'm just a little tired."

Sara's eyes lingered on her grandmother's face. Obaachan always had lots of energy, but she was getting older.

"Maybe it's time for me to retire," Obaachan said, as if reading Sara's mind.

"No!" Sara said. "You're not old, Obaachan!"

Obaachan smiled. "Maybe not so old," she said. "But I can't keep baking if there are no customers to bake for."

Sara knew her grandmother was right. The bakery couldn't stay in business if half the things Obaachan baked were unsold at the end of the day. Sara was sure business would get better again, if she could just find Maneki Neko.

CHAPTER SEVEN
Night Cat

Sara stayed overnight at her grandmother's apartment again. She lay awake in bed long after she heard Obaachan's soft snoring coming from the other room. She remembered the black cat she'd seen in the yard the night before. Maybe the cat was there again.

Climbing silently from bed, Sara peered out the window. The yard was dark, still and empty. But as she watched, the black cat stepped out from the shadows. It sat for several moments, motionless as a statue. Then it looked up at her and raised one paw.

Again, Sara was surprised by how much the cat reminded her of Maneki Neko. She felt a fresh stab of loss in her chest. Maneki Neko had been like a real cat to her. Tears came to Sara's eyes, and she blinked them away. When her eyes cleared, the cat was gone.

Sara wondered who the cat belonged to. Had someone shut it outside by accident? Was it lost? Was someone looking for it? She thought about what people did when they lost a real cat. They phoned animal shelters, put up *Missing Cat* posters. If Maneki Neko was a real cat, that's what she would do.

Sara froze. That was it. She would make *Missing Cat* posters for Maneki Neko.

CHAPTER EIGHT
Inspiration

When Sara got up the next morning, Obaachan had been baking for several hours. The smell of fresh buns wafted up the stairs and filled the apartment. Once she was ready for school, Sara went down to the kitchen to join Obaachan.

Obaachan smiled when she saw Sara and slid a final tray of buns into the oven. She closed the oven door and wiped her hands on her red and blue pin-striped apron.

On the little table at the back of the kitchen, there was a bowl of fresh fruit and a pot of tea. Sara set out plates and cutlery. Obaachan brought over a plate of steaming buns and a jar of strawberry jam.

"Did you have a good sleep?" Obaachan asked as she sat down at the table.

"Yes," Sara said. She wanted to ask Obaachan about the cat she had seen in the backyard. Maybe Obaachan knew who owned it. But Sara thought talking about the cat would remind Obaachan of Maneki Neko.

Obaachan poured tea into two handleless cups and sliced up an apple. She set the apple slices on Sara's plate. Sara grinned. Obaachan's quick fingers had cut each slice into a rabbit. She loved how Obaachan always made things a little bit special.

"When are you going to make animal buns again?" Sara asked.

"I don't know," Obaachan said. "I used to make them on Saturdays when things were busier."

Sara pictured the animal buns with their tiny bun ears and noses. Obaachan's customers used to love them.

Sara thought about making the *Missing Cat* posters. Sometimes people offered a reward for the return of a missing pet, but she didn't think Obaachan had any extra money for that. Then Sara had an idea.

"Obaachan," she asked. "Could you make some animal buns this Saturday?"

"They are a lot of work," Obaachan said.

"Please," Sara said. "I was thinking of asking Jake to come by."

Her grandmother smiled. "That boy does seem to like my baking," she said. Her back straightened. "All right. I'll make some."

Sara had one more favor to ask. She hesitated, then plunged ahead.

"Can you make them cat buns?" she asked.

CHAPTER NINE

The Plan

Sara thought her plan through as she walked to school. If someone took Maneki Neko, she hoped the statue was still in the neighborhood somewhere. Maybe one of their neighbors had seen it.

Sara had a hard time concentrating on schoolwork that morning. At recess she asked her teacher for some paper and stayed inside to work. By the time recess ended, Sara had finished three small posters. It wasn't much, but it was a start.

"What are you doing?" Jake asked as he sat down beside her. "You missed recess."

Sara passed him a poster. In large letters at the top of the page was the word *Missing.* Underneath that was a drawing of a cat. Sara had included a nice long tail even though the statue didn't seem to have one.

"Is this your lucky cat?" he asked, nodding at the drawing. "It looks real."

"Yeah," Sara said. Sometimes Maneki Neko did seem real.

"How many posters are you going to make?" Jake asked.

"As many as I can," Sara said.

"That will take forever!" Jake laughed.

Sara frowned. Was he making fun of her? She tried to snatch the poster back, but Jake shifted out of her reach.

"You need to photocopy them," he said.

Sara gaped at Jake. Why hadn't she thought of that? "Do you think I can use the school photocopier?" she asked.

Jake shrugged. "You could ask at lunch. I'll come with you."

"Thanks," Sara said. She picked up the rest of the posters. If Jake was willing to help copy the posters, would he help with the next step? Their teacher walked to the front of the room. Sara would have to ask Jake quickly or wait until lunch. She took a deep breath.

"Do you want to help me put the posters up after school?" she asked.

Jake didn't answer right away. Then he shrugged. Just as the teacher called for silence, he said, "Okay."

"We can visit the bakery again too," Sara said. "I'm sure my grandma will let us pick whatever we like."

Sara snuck one sideways glance at Jake. She wasn't sure, but it looked like there was a drop of drool at the corner of his mouth.

CHAPTER TEN

Poster Power

After school, Sara stuffed the posters in her backpack. Mrs. Chew, the school secretary, had let her photocopy a whole stack when Sara said she needed them to help find her cat.

Jake opened his backpack to reveal the tape dispenser and stapler he had borrowed from the school. "All set for Operation Cat Find," he said.

Sara looked at her watch. "Our mission starts at three fifteen," she said, deepening her voice to sound like a secret agent.

"We could synchronize our watches," Jake said. "Except I don't have a watch."

They both laughed. But Sara felt a twinge of uncertainty. She felt bad about letting Mrs. Chew believe Maneki Neko was a real cat. Did it matter that Maneki Neko was a statue? If someone had seen the statue, she hoped they would also see the posters.

Jake stopped beside a bus stop.

"We should put up a poster here," he said. "People will read it while they wait for the bus."

"Good idea," Sara said. She was glad Jake had agreed to help.

Sara unzipped her backpack and slipped out a poster. She stepped inside the bus shelter and held the poster in place above the bench while Jake stuck on the tape.

"Let's put one on this telephone pole too," Jake said.

They stapled the poster to the pole.

"What does that mean?" Jake asked, pointing to words near the bottom of the poster.

If you have any information,
come to Sakura Bakery on Saturday
for a REWARD!

Sara grinned. "You will have to come by to find out," she said.

They continued down the street, putting up posters along the way. At the corner store, a block from Obaachan's bakery, Sara asked the clerk if she could put a poster in the store window.

"Go ahead," said the clerk. "I hope you find your cat."

They stopped at the Laundromat next.

"I haven't been to the bakery in quite a while," Mr. Leonardo, the Laundromat owner, said. "Does your grandma still make those delicious curry buns?"

"She does," Sara said. "Drop by on Saturday. She's making something special."

Mr. Leonardo rubbed his chin thoughtfully. "I might do that," he said.

After Sara and Jake taped a poster on the window, Sara thanked Mr. Leonardo and headed for the door.

"I'll be sure to tell my customers to watch out for that cat," he called after her.

Sara felt hopeful. Maybe her plan would work.

CHAPTER ELEVEN
Waiting Game

When there was only one poster left, Sara stopped. She wanted to save it for the bakery door.

As they approached the bakery, Sara saw something move in the back alley. She thought she glimpsed a black tail disappear behind a building. She wondered where the nighttime cat was. Had it found its way home? And where was Maneki Neko? Would she and Obaachan ever see their lucky cat statue again?

Sara taped the last poster on the bakery door, and then she and Jake went inside. Obaachan had two chocolate-chip melon-pan waiting for them.

The buns were round with a cracked surface like a cantaloupe melon. The outside was a layer of crispy cookie, but the inside was soft sweet bun.

"This is good!" Jake said, his mouth full of bun.

Obaachan beamed at Jake, and Sara smiled too.

After Jake had gone home, Obaachan locked up the bakery. Sara's dad came to pick her up.

"Can't I stay at Obaachan's tonight?" Sara asked.

"Your mom and I haven't seen you all week," her dad said. "Don't you miss us?" He made a sad puppy face.

"Maybe," Sara teased. She wanted to see her parents, but she didn't want to leave Obaachan on her own.

"Don't worry about me," Obaachan said. "I'll be fine."

Sara thought about the nighttime cat. Would it appear again tonight? Would the cat notice she wasn't there? What about her plan? Tomorrow was Friday. She needed to be at the bakery Saturday morning.

"Can I stay with Obaachan tomorrow night?" she asked.

Her dad frowned. "Don't you want to be home for the weekend?" he asked. "Obaachan can come and visit us there."

"But Obaachan's making cat buns on Saturday, and my friend's coming over," she added.

"Okay," Dad said, holding up his hands in surrender. "You can stay with Obaachan tomorrow. But come home tonight. Your mom's starting to forget what you look like."

CHAPTER TWELVE
Ready or Not

At school on Friday Sara tried to focus on her schoolwork. During lunch she played soccer with Jake, his friend Kevin and several other kids. It felt good to run around and have fun.

"Don't forget to come to the bakery tomorrow," Sara reminded Jake at the end of the day.

"I'll be there," Jake promised. He was going to Kevin's house after school. She hoped he wouldn't forget about Saturday.

Sara joined a group of kids walking home but lagged behind them. What if Jake had so much fun with Kevin, he forgot to come to the bakery?

What if Kevin asked Jake to come to his house on Saturday too?

Sara paused at the bus stop where she and Jake had put up the first posters. The poster inside the shelter had been torn off. Sara's heart fell. What if all the posters were gone?

She looked at the telephone pole and sighed with relief. The poster was still there.

Sara hurried the rest of the way to the bakery, scanning for posters. Most of them were still in place. But there was no way of knowing if anyone had read them. What if the posters didn't work and no one showed up at the bakery on Saturday?

Sara helped Obaachan until it was time to close. Then she and Obaachan ate supper together. Sara was quiet.

"Are you feeling okay?" Obaachan asked Sara at bedtime.

"I'm fine," Sara said. "Just sleepy." She didn't want to tell Obaachan she was worried about tomorrow. Obaachan knew about the posters, but Sara hadn't told her about the reward and how she hoped it would introduce new customers to Obaachan's delicious baking.

"Don't forget to make the cat buns," Sara said.

"I won't," Obaachan said, giving Sara a hug.

The only thing left to do was wait for the morning. Sara got ready for bed and turned out the light. Once her eyes had adjusted to the dark, she went to the window.

Thin clouds drifted across the night sky like long fingers hiding the face of the moon. Down below, the yard was shadowed and still. There was no sign of the black cat. Disappointment tugged at Sara. If the stray cat was gone, maybe Maneki Neko was gone too. Her plan felt silly.

Sara started to turn away from the window, then stopped. Had something moved under the cherry tree?

She looked again, but the yard was empty. Had she imagined it? She stared into the yard, but there was no movement and no cat.

Sara climbed into bed and pulled up the covers. "Maneki Neko, where are you?" she whispered into the dark.

CHAPTER THIRTEEN
Reward

In the morning, Sara helped Obaachan carry the fresh buns and pastries from the kitchen to the bakery.

"How do they look?" Obaachan asked as she held up a tray filled with smiling cats, each with one raised paw.

"Perfect!" said Sara. But she did not feel as happy as she sounded. Her posters told people to come to the bakery on Saturday if they had any information about the missing cat statue. Would anyone show up?

At nine o'clock, Obaachan unlocked the door. No one was waiting to come in.

Then, to Sara's surprise, Mr. Leonardo from the Laundromat bustled through the door, waving Sara's poster.

"I'm sorry," he said. "I saw the cat, but I couldn't catch it."

Sara's forehead wrinkled in confusion. There must be a mistake.

"But our missing cat is a statue," Sara explained. "Not real."

Obaachan stepped forward to look at the poster in Mr. Leonardo's hand.

"But, I thought—" Mr. Leonardo sputtered, pointing at the poster. "Isn't this a real cat?"

Sara's face burned, and a lump formed in her throat. Her Maneki Neko drawing looked too real, and her wording hadn't been clear.

"Reward?" Obaachan asked, still looking at the poster in confusion.

"The cat buns," Sara whispered.

Understanding spread across Obaachan's face, and she smiled at Mr. Leonardo. "Thank you for coming," she told him. "Please take one of our special buns as a gift."

With a bow, she presented him with one of the cat buns wrapped in a paper napkin.

"That looks wonderful," Mr. Leonardo said. He admired the bun before taking a big bite.

"Delicious!" he said. "Can I buy some to take home?"

"Of course," Obaachan said.

She slipped behind the counter as the bell on the bakery door jangled. Two young women walked into the store.

"I think I saw that cat in the poster," one of them said.

The other woman's eyes roved over the rows of fresh baked items. "Those look good," she said.

"Have a lucky cat bun," Obaachan said, smiling and holding out buns to the women. "It's a thank-you special."

While Mr. Leonardo placed his order, Sara explained to the women that the missing cat was not real.

"But I saw it walk right up to the bakery door," the first woman said. "It looked exactly like the cat in the picture."

"That's right," said the second woman. "It was black with brown spots."

Sara frowned. It sounded like the cat she had seen in the backyard.

The bakery door jangled. Sara looked up to see Jake and his mother.

"Mmm, it smells good in here," Jake's mom said.

"Hey!" Jake called.

He stepped inside the door, and Sara saw he was holding something in his arms. She could hardly believe her eyes.

It was Maneki Neko.

CHAPTER FOURTEEN
Lucky Cat

"You found him!" Sara cheered.

Obaachan looked up from behind the counter, craning her head to see past the customers. She saw Jake and the lucky cat, and her cheeks rounded with the biggest smile Sara had ever seen.

Sara hurried to take Maneki Neko from Jake. Carefully, she placed the statue in the window. Then she rubbed the top of his head for good luck.

"Where did you find him?" Sara asked Jake.

"When my mom and I got here, I saw a cat sitting beside the bakery," Jake said. "It looked just like the cat in your drawing, but it was real."

"We saw it too," said one of the young women who had come in ahead of Jake.

"It ran around the back, and I followed it," Jake said. "When I got to the backyard I couldn't see the cat anymore. But the statue was sitting on the ground under a tree."

Sara's mouth dropped open. Had Jake seen the nighttime cat? And how had Maneki Neko ended up in the backyard?

"Oh my!" Obaachan said.

Sara turned to see Obaachan put her hands to her head. Obaachan's face looked a little red.

"I just remembered," said Obaachan. "When I was cleaning the bakery the other night, I took Maneki Neko outside to give him a good wash."

So that's what had happened. Sara was sure she had looked in the backyard, but she mustn't have looked very well. Suddenly, Sara felt foolish. But the feeling soon vanished when the bell above the front

door jangled again and another person entered the bakery. Before the door had time to close, the bell jangled again.

"I'll be right back," Sara said to Jake.

Sara hurried to the kitchen to bring out another tray of lucky cat buns. It looked like lots of people had seen Maneki Neko's look-alike. They were going to need lots of buns.

In the window of the bakery, Maneki Neko sat in his old spot, as if he'd never left. On his head and sides, the familiar black paint was worn away and patches of brown clay showed through. One paw was raised, beckoning people into the bakery.

Sara handed out cat buns to all the customers. She smiled at Obaachan and then at Jake.

Maneki Neko was back. And so was the bakery's good luck.

JACQUELINE PEARCE grew up on Vancouver Island, exploring nature, playing road hockey and other sports, reading books, writing stories and drawing. She has always been fascinated with local history, and her first three novels, *The Reunion*, *Discovering Emily* and *Emily's Dream*, all tell stories about Vancouver Island's past. Her interest in other countries and cultures, nature and animals also makes its way into her novels and short stories. Jacqueline has degrees in English literature and environmental studies. She currently lives on the edge of a ravine near Vancouver, British Columbia, with her husband, daughter, dog and two cats.